FIVE OAKS RANCH

A Christmas To Remember

Stephanie Payne Hurt

A CHRISTMAS TO REMEMBER©2015
Stephanie Payne Hurt
Five Oaks Ranch Series
Horseshoe Publishing
Cover Designer: Kaleigh Payne
Any person mentioned in this book is not based on any person, living or nonliving.
This book is a work of fiction. This book may not be reproduced, transmitted, or stored in whole or in part by any means, including graphic, electronic, or mechanical without the express written consent of the publisher.

Sign up for my newsletter at www.stephaniehurtauthor.com to keep up with upcoming events and new releases.

Also, come by and join my Street Team for chances to win books, get to read chapters before their release and get to know me on a more personal level. All the information is on my website!

A note to my readers:

The Five Oaks Ranch series has been really special for me. It was about the Cauthen siblings and this book is a touching story of their parent's great love as Maggie gets married.

Another reason it's special to me is the name Cauthen. My dad's mother was a Cauthen before she married and I wanted to share some of the love of our family. At the end of the book, you'll find a special section of recipes. Most of these were pulled from the yellowing pages of my grandmother's notebook. They were written in her handwriting and are very special to me.

I hope you've enjoyed this series as much as I have. Here's to a great Christmas for all of you and a blessed New Year. I appreciate each and every one of my readers!

Love and happiness,

Stephanie Payne Hurt

PROLOGUE

Christmas 1984

Bridget Cauthen sat under the Christmas tree gazing up at the lights. This time of year was special for her. Today was her second anniversary with Grantland. To make it more special, they were expecting their first child, a boy.

Grantland walked into the room, stopping to admire the sight of his beautiful wife, looking up at the tree. He couldn't help but smile as she unconsciously rubbed her large belly. The excitement of their first child filled the house.

He sat down beside her, handing her a mug of hot chocolate. After two years he'd learned how she like it, with only seven small marshmallows and a spoon of whipped cream. Bridget eagerly took the mug with a smile.

"Just as I love it." She winked at him as she took a sip, sighing.

"It's part of the marriage thing, learn what your lady loves." Grantland put his arm around her shoulders, pulling her close as they sat enjoying the peace of the moment.

Outside sleet lashed at the windows, but inside it was cozy and warm. The fire crackled behind them as the clock chimed eight times. Grantland stood up, pulling Bridget up beside him.

He pushed the play button on the cassette player. "Would you like to dance my love?" Bowing in front of her, making her giggle.

"Why Grantland Cauthen, how you sweep me off my feet?" She said in her best Scarlett impression, fluttering her eyes.

"I aim to please." He pulled her close, holding their hands clasped between them. They slowly made their way around in front of the fireplace. The Christmas music flowing around them.

Bridget laid her head on his chest, closing her eyes. Their love grew deeper every moment they were together. The child she carried would be filled with so much love.

As the years went by, their love added three more boys, then in 1995 the Lord blessed them with a little girl. Her brothers adored her beyond words.

Bridget and Grantland stood watching the boys taking turns holding their little sister in front of the Christmas tree. It was touching the way they were with her.

"We filled our children with as much love as we could." Bridget smiled through her tears.

"Yes, my love, we did. It stems from our

special love." He kissed her sweetly, then looking down into her eyes. "You've blessed me with five beautiful children, each unique and loved. I love you Bridget Cauthen."

Bridget wrapped her arms around her husband. "I love you more Grantland Cauthen."

Chapter 1

Maggie sat staring out the window as the leaves fell like rain in the front yard. Her wedding was over a month away. This made her heart skip a beat.

Her thoughts went to Dalton, her future husband, as a smile spread across her face. She was a lucky woman to get such a wonderful man. Dalton was handsome, strong, smart, sexy, everything you'd want in a husband. It took her four over protective brothers to get used to the idea of them, but when they saw how happy she was, it changed them.

They spent every moment together, trying to make plans for their future. Deep down she was struggling with the fact that she'd be leaving the Five Oaks Ranch. This had been her home all of her life. It was where she learned to ride a horse, fell out of a tree and broke her arm, there were more firsts than she could even think of. But it would always hold a special place in her heart.

A hand on her shoulder had her turning from the thoughts running through her head. Behind Maggie, her mother stood smiling as though she knew what was going through her mind.

"I saw that smile turn down slightly." Bridget Cauthen said as she put her arm around Maggie's shoulders.

"Guess my mind is in overdrive." Maggie leaned into her mom as they walked to the kitchen.

"Well, let's get some pumpkin spice tea and talk about it." They worked together making the tea and grabbing some of the tea cakes that Maggie made earlier that day.

"I can't believe the wedding is a little over a month away. It's coming up so fast and I don't feel like I have anything ready." Maggie let out a sigh as she sipped the spicy tea. Her heart was heavy as doubt tried to fill her.

"Don't worry, everything will fall into place nicely. It's funny, all brides feel this way as their wedding's approach." Bridget took a sip of tea as she saw something cross her daughter's eyes. "But there's something else, isn't there?"

Maggie looked up at her mother with surprise. She'd tried to hide her emotions lately, especially from Dalton, although he'd figured it out months ago and supported her with his love.

"I guess it's the fact that I'll be leaving Five Oaks. It's starting to really dig in." Tears started to well up in her eyes as the thought ran through again.

"It's not like you'll never come back here.

Now you'll have a ranch to run and that will soon have you too busy to think about Five Oaks."

"That's what Dalton said. He's been so supportive and loving about this." Maggie smiled as a single tear slipped down her cheek.

Bridget smiled, "I felt the same way when I left my parent's home to come here to Five Oaks, of course then it was just the Cauthen farm. But once we were married and our new life started, the love we had made up for the sadness of leaving home. I was home here, at the ranch."

Ridge walked in and stopped when he saw Maggie wipe her tears away. "What's wrong?" He was instantly concerned.

Maggie giggled, "I'm fine, just feeling emotional about leaving Five Oaks."

He put his arms around her, kissing the back of her head. "You're not leaving Five Oaks, just moving to another great ranch. You'll always be a part of this place, that'll never change sis."

She reached up, placing her hand on his

arm. "Thanks Ridge. I guess I'm being silly, huh?"

"Nope, just being realistic. It's a big step to leave the place you were raised, but you have a good man and a home to keep up." Ridge reached out and took the last tea cake from her plate. "I know it's me you'll miss more than anything, but you can come see me any time you want to."

Maggie laughed out loud and hit his hand as he snatched the cookie. "Ridge there's something seriously wrong with you." She stood up and put her cup in the sink.

Chase walked in, hearing her words. "You're just now figuring that one out. Come on sis, you know he's always had something wrong with him." He leaned down and kissed his mother's cheek.

Ridge grunted, "Maggie was just saying how much she'll miss me once she's married and living at Dalton's." He leaned on the counter with a satisfied grin.

"Excuse me, she'll be missing me, not you." Chase grabbed Maggie as she started past him. "Isn't that right Mags?"

"Mom, I think I'll be just fine at another ranch. I wasn't thinking about the fact that my four brothers wouldn't be there." She giggled when Chase groaned, then tickled her side.

Bridget Cauthen smiled as she watched her grown children acting half their age. She was proud of her children. Each of them had their own personality, but together, they were so much alike. They turned out to be wonderful adults, filled with intelligence, common sense and love.

"Alright children, get out of my kitchen so I can get started on dinner." She smiled as they went out the door, pushing one another and laughing. It was amazing how well they got along.

Ridge, Chase and Maggie walked out on the front porch as Dalton drove up to the front walk. "I wasn't expecting him to come by this afternoon." Maggie said as she watched him walk up the path.

"What has you over here in the middle of the day?" Ridge grasped his friends hand as he spoke.

"I thought I'd steal my fiancé away since it's such a nice day." Dalton wrapped his arms around Maggie.

"That's a wonderful idea. She's been a real brat all day." Chase said as he moved out of Maggie's reach.

Dalton laughed, then planted a kiss on her lips. "Good thing I finished chores early then."

"Where are we going?" Maggie's eyes danced with happiness as she gave her brothers a warning look. Her earlier doubts slipping away as Dalton held her close. This was all she needed to make her feel comfortable and convinced her nerves were making her crazy.

"Not telling you, it's a surprise." He kissed her again, which earned a groan from her brothers.

"Get a room you two." Ridge said as he

walked down the steps and headed toward the barn. Then he called back over his shoulder. "That was a joke by the way." His tone told them he was serious.

Chase slapped Dalton's shoulder, "Definitely a joke. So, you two kids have fun." He followed Ridge across the yard.

She smiled as Dalton grasped her hand and pulled her toward his truck. He drove out to his ranch, which made her wonder what the surprise was. She'd figured he was taking her out for dinner. Then as they pulled up in front of the house she laughed out loud.

There sitting on the front porch with a huge red bow was a blue tick hound. The dog barked as they got out of the truck, the sound echoing across the yard. Maggie almost ran to where the dog patiently waited.

"Where did he come from?" She wrapped her arms around the dog with a giggle. This was one of her wishes, to have a blue tick.

"It's the first of many wedding gifts to come." He tapped her nose with his finger, "By the way, I plan on spoiling you, shamelessly."

The dog seemed to enjoy the attention, but in a patient way. Maggie giggled as she continued to hug the dog, finally pulling it into her lap. She was beyond touched at the thoughtful gift. Then she smiled even broader as she remembered a conversation they had back in the summer as they lay under the stars. Dalton wanted to know some of her wishes. A thrill came into her as she remembered that night. He revealed some of his wishes and Maggie was already in the process of acquiring some things.

It was amazing how they thought alike. Dalton watched with pleasure as she loved on the dog. He knew this present would being her complete joy. Maggie was easy to please and he loved that about her. She wasn't your typical woman that needed to be pampered. Maggie was just Maggie, no frills, no fancy nails, just the beautiful woman before him.

Dalton was able to extract her from the dog about thirty minutes later. He pulled her into his arms for a long kiss. "I'm glad you like your present." His voice was husky as he kissed her again.

"I love it. You're too good to me." Her eyes filled with love as she gazed at her husband to be.

Chapter 2

The weather grew colder. Maggie was still uncertain about a wedding dress. She'd been to every bridal shop within a fifty-mile radius. All she wanted was a simple dress, but everything she saw was too lacy, or too many pearls. That wasn't her at all.

Bridget knew her daughter was struggling. One day after they'd returned from a dress shopping trip, she made a decision. "Maggie, I have something to show you."

Maggie followed her mother up to her

parent's bedroom. She was curious what her mother was up to. As they walked into the bedroom, her mother's smile broadened.

"I know you've been having a hard time finding the wedding dress that's right for you." Her mother knelt down in front of her cedar chest that had set at the foot of the bed as long as Maggie could remember. "I've been waiting to see if you find what you're looking for before I made a suggestion."

A gasp escaped Maggie's lips as she realized what her mother was pulling from the chest. She pulled a white box out that had been nestled in the bottom, underneath her mother's treasured items from her marriage and five children. As her mother placed the box on the floor, tears formed in Maggie's eyes.

"It's old, but after looking at the dresses today, it's back in style." Bridget opened the box, revealing the white dress within.

Maggie grasped the simple white satin

dress carefully, pulling it from the box. It had a round neckline without being covered with lace and pearls. The waistline was princess cut, which flowed into a pleated skirt that hung to the floor. It was simple elegance.

"Oh mom, it's the perfect dress." The tears she'd held at bay, slipped past her lashes as she held the dress in front of her to look in the mirror. "It's been a long time since you showed it to me. I'd forgotten how beautiful it is."

"Now, go try it on and let's see if we need to make any alterations." Bridget wiped a single tear from her cheek. Her baby was getting married. It was hard to believe that all five of her children would be out of the house. When had time slipped away. It seemed like only yesterday they were running through the house, screaming and laughing, now they were grown and making their own families.

When Maggie came out of the bathroom, Bridget covered her mouth. The beauty before her was beyond words. Her daughter was the most beautiful sight. She circled Maggie, checking the fit.

"Mom, this is the perfect dress. It's everything I've been looking for." She spun around, giggling.

A knock at the door stopped her. Bridget walked over and peeked out the door, then opened it wider as Grantland, Maggie's father stepped inside. When his eyes landed on Maggie, he smiled. Walking over to his daughter, he leaned over and kissed her cheek.

"You're beautiful sweetheart." He turned, putting his arm around Bridget. "This dress brings back some special memories."

Maggie walked over to the antique mirror that stood beside the bathroom. She looked at herself and couldn't believe her eyes.

"Tell me about that day dad." She turned back to look at her parents.

He looked down at his wife with love, "It

was the coldest Christmas on record at the time. I was afraid that I wouldn't be able to marry your mama on Christmas Eve as we'd planned. You see, she had to come from town and the roads were starting to ice over. The phone lines were down, so I couldn't call her. It was the longest day, waiting for her to get here."

Bridget leaned her head on his arm. "I was coming if I had to walk all the way in the icy weather."

"The preacher arrived thirty minutes early and still no bride. I was getting nervous when the door opened and there she stood. The most beautiful sight in the world. She was wrapped in a red shawl. I'll never forget the look on her face when our eyes met. I knew beyond any doubt that what we had together would get us through anything."

"So you made it through the icy weather to marry the man you loved." Maggie watched her parents kiss each other as the memories flooded them. "Such a sweet way to start your life together."

"Oh, it gets better. Your dad forgot where he put my ring and we spent over an hour looking for the it." Bridget looked up at her husband and laughed. "He put his hand in his pocket to get his handkerchief and out popped the ring. He'd put it in his pocket for safe keeping and with his nerves, totally forgot."

Maggie laughed out loud. "Dad, you really didn't do that?"

"See what your mother did to my mind." He hugged his wife tighter. "She blew my mind the first time I set eyes on her in kindergarten and every day since then. I've been walking around in a haze most of my life, but that's fine with me. She keeps me straight."

"Now you'll be married in the same spot as we were." Bridget walked over to the cedar chest and reached in, looking for something. "Ah, here we are." She looked up at Grantland, "Do you remember this?"

She held up a handkerchief with the initial C on it. Grantland touched the item with a grin. "You kept this all these years Bridget, that's so you."

"It was from our wedding day." Bridget held it to her face lovingly. "The most wonderful day of my life, other than the day each of you children were born. I keep everything that means something, like this handkerchief that your dad gave me as we stood before the preacher."

"Glad I had it in my pocket because you were about the flood the den." He laughed and hugged her to him. "I wouldn't take anything for those tears of joy."

"Where did you go on your honeymoon?" Maggie asked as she held her hair up, seeing how it would look. She realized she didn't know that much about the time around her parent's marriage.

"Our first night was spent in town at the hotel. Remember the one that burned a couple of years ago. Then we drove to Florida and spent four days running on the beach and eating our fill of seafood. It was warmer down there."

"When did you move in here at the main house?" Maggie said as she turned to smile at her parents.

"We stayed in the cabin beside the house. It's where we lived until just before Ridge was born. It was a cozy first home and we made it our own little love nest, didn't we love." Bridget grasped Grantland's hand.

"You have a romantic love story." Maggie said as she walked into the bathroom to change. When she came out, her dad was gone. "Where did dad go?"

"He wanted to get something down from the attic for you." Bridget said as she put everything back in the chest, closing it with a contented smile.

"What?" Maggie was curious.

Her dad walked in with a beautiful

wedding ring quilt draped over his arm. "This is for you and Dalton. Your great grandmother Cauthen made this for your mother and I for a wedding present. Now it's time to pass it down to our youngest child." The quilt had a creamy background, with dark red, green and brown rings on it.

Maggie reached out to take the quilt, pulling it to her nose. She smiled as the scent of cedar filled her senses. "It's beautiful and such a special gift."

Chapter 3

The Thanksgiving meal was full of conversation about the wedding. All of the women were discussing the wedding tree that was planned. Since Maggie and Dalton were getting married in front of the Christmas tree, she wanted a special tree. It would have no ordinary ornaments, but cherished items and mementos.

Maggie was quiet as dessert was served. Dalton watched her as she toyed with her pie. She put the fork down, looking out the window in deep thought. He knew as the wedding drew near, nerves were taking over. It was getting to him too, but knowing they'd be together forever made him anxious.

Dalton touched her cheek, drawing her gaze around to him. "Let's go for a walk."

"Alright." She stood up, taking her untouched pie to the kitchen. When she walked back into the hallway, he was waiting with their jackets.

They walked for a little while, not talking. She was enjoying the cool air as he was enjoying just being with her without the whole Cauthen clan watching. Some days he felt uncomfortable just holding her hand in their presence. Chase and Luke seemed alright with their engagement, but the Ridge and Oakley were too quiet.

Maggie stopped just before they reached the back pasture. She hadn't realized how far they'd gone. The blue sky overhead was beautiful as little wispy clouds floated over slowly as though they were lazy.

"Dalton, I know I've been acting weird lately." She didn't look at him as she spoke.

"Look Maggie, I understand your nerves. I've felt them myself. Some days I look at you and can't believe your mine. It's beyond my comprehension why you'd want someone like me." He leaned his arms on the fence beside them.

She turned, smiling. "Dalton, you're everything I want in a man, smart, witty, funny, handsome and you love the ranch life as much as I do. Why wouldn't I want you as my husband?" Placing her hand on his muscular arm, she leaned her head against him.

"We'll be married in a month." He said as he looked down at her. "I remember watching you race your horse across this field, not a care in the world. You were fearless as a girl and you're fearless now. So what has you so upset my love?" Kissing the top of her head, he felt like a king knowing this wonderful woman would be his wife.

A groan escaped her lips, "It's all coming

so fast. The day we marry will be the day I leave Five Oaks, the home I've known all my life. I guess you could say I'm a little sad about that, but I'm also excited about our new life at your ranch."

He reached out and lifted her chin, so she was looking at him. "Correction, our ranch. It will be our ranch my sweet Maggie. It will be your home."

"And I can't wait for that day. Why am I acting so silly about this?" A tear made its way down her cheek.

Dalton wiped away the tear as another slipped over his finger. "Don't cry sweetheart. It's not silly. Do you want to hear something?" When she nodded he continued. "When I was deployed, I wanted to cry. Leaving my home was the hardest thing I've ever done, but can you imagine me sitting among all those brave soldiers letting my feelings out."

She giggled at the thought of the looks he would've gotten. "That would have been a little awkward." Maggie entwined her hand with his, bringing it to her lips. "I love you beyond words."

He pulled her into his arms, kissing her with a passion he'd held back for so long. Her arms went around his neck as the kiss deepened to a level that warmed their souls. A sound behind them brought them back down to earth.

A doe stood just beyond them, watching carefully. Then she ran across the pasture, effortlessly jumping the fence beyond them. She turned back to look at them once more, before disappearing into the wood line.

Dalton pulled her back against him. "Sorry for the interruption, that was beginning to get interesting."

Maggie turned in his arms, "Maybe we should head back to the house."

They walked in the front door, hearing laughter in the kitchen. The family was packed in the kitchen, watching Beau walking across the floor, carrying a large sugar cookie. When he saw his aunt, he made his way over to her. Maggie picked him up, kissing his plump cheek. "What have you been up to?"

"Where have you two been?" Chase leaned toward Maggie with a sly grin.

"For a walk." She left it at that as she blushed under the scrutiny of her four brothers. Why did they make her feel like she'd done something wrong? Looking around at them, she hugged Beau to her.

"Nice, cold day for a walk, but a few kisses in the pasture can warm things up." Luke turned to the couple with a grin.

"How did you know that?" Maggie shot him a hard look. "Did you follow us?"

"No Mags, it's evident on Dalton's face and lips." He grinned as everyone looked toward Dalton. His lips were the same color as Maggie's lipstick and he had several kisses on his cheeks.

Mrs. Cauthen knew it was about to get heated, so she held up her hands. "Alright boys, out of the kitchen. We need to wash up these dishes."

Maggie handed Beau to Ridge as he passed her. When Luke started by, she reached out to pop his arm, but he darted away from her. "You're so bad."

Luke laughed, "I wasn't the one necking in the pasture." He gave her a quick wink as he went out the door.

"Ignore him." Rachel said as she turned the water on in the sink.

Together, the family sat that evening watching old family movies. The movies were around the time that Maggie was born and up to her second birthday. She was touched how her brothers watched over her, not letting her fall down or get into trouble. Looking around at her family, she knew this would always be home, but it was time for her to make a home of her own, with Dalton.

The love her parents shared was something

most people didn't get a chance at. She felt like she had that kind of love with Dalton. It would be wonderful passing down that love to their children one day.

Chapter 4

Two weeks before the Christmas wedding, the family gave Maggie and Dalton a surprise shower. It brought Maggie to tears as everyone hugged them. The gifts were all special items for the house. Even though Dalton's house was set up already, they wanted to have some new things.

Mr. & Mrs. Cauthen gave them a honeymoon trip to a cabin in the mountains of Montana. Dalton couldn't believe their generosity. He'd always wanted to go to Montana, which was one of the things he and Maggie had in common.

Ridge and Mallory decided to give them a nights stay at the bed and breakfast just out of town for the first night. Oakley and Ellen gave them new cookware, which made Dalton laugh, saying his were in dire need of replacing. Chase and Cara presented them with new towels and linens. Luke and Rachel's gift was a 12 place setting of Maggie's favorite dishes.

Several of their friends came over with gifts. The food was holiday oriented with poinsettia cupcakes and Christmas cookies. They even had hot chocolate punch. Maggie sat in among their gifts with a smile.

After most of the guests left, the guys loaded up their gifts in Dalton's truck. Maggie followed him to his house to help unload. They made a couple of trips to get everything in the house. The temperature outside was just above freezing as Dalton built a fire as Maggie fixed them two cups of coffee. They collapsed in front of the fire. It had been a busy day.

Dalton held Maggie close as they watched the fire pop and crackle. She couldn't wait until they could do sit by the fire every evening. It was getting harder and harder to leave him. He walked her to the truck, holding her close before she drove out of the gates. He watched her taillights, knowing it was only two weeks until she'd be staying with him, not going away.

As Maggie drove home, her mind completely on the upcoming wedding that she didn't notice the deer on the side of the road until it darted in front of her. She swerved out of the way, her truck running up into the woods, hitting a tree. Her body was flung forward from the impact.

***

Ridge reached in the dark for his cell phone as it vibrated. He looked at the clock, seeing it was two a.m. His heart began to race as he realized it must be an emergency.

"Hello." He said in a rush, not wanting to hear what was wrong.

"Ridge, it's Dalton. Sorry man, but I'm worried about Maggie, she never called to say she was home. I didn't want to upset your parents if she forgot to call." Dalton's voice sounded upset, making Ridge sit up.

Mallory sat up, putting her hand on Ridge's arm. "What's wrong?"

He put a hand up, holding her back for a moment. "Did you try her cell?"

"Yes, but she didn't answer it." Dalton was grabbing his keys as he spoke. "I'm heading toward the ranch, if you'll start this way. She may have broken down or ..." He didn't finish the sentence, not wanting to think about the alternative.

"Hold on before you start this way. Let me drive down to the house and see if her trucks home. I'll call you in a few minutes." He jumped up, pulling his jeans and sweat shirt on.

"What's wrong Ridge?" Mallory said as she climbed out of bed.

"Maggie didn't call Dalton to say she was home. Now she's not answering her phone. She probably just forgot, but I'll go check." He kissed her before he ran out the door.

On the drive past the barns toward the main house, his heart was beating fast. If her truck wasn't parked out front he'd panic. As he rounded the last barn and the house came into sight his heart sank. Her truck wasn't in her usual place.

Picking up his phone from the console, he dialed Dalton. "Head this way, she's not home."

"Crap, I'm heading out the door now." Dalton ran to his truck, spinning in the gravel as he sped out of the yard. What could've happened? It was so cold out tonight. If she broke down, would she be able to stay warm?

Dalton drove toward Five Oaks in the direction she always went. His adrenaline was on overload as he saw Ridge's headlights up ahead. They stopped beside one another.

"I didn't see her, did you?" Dalton said as

he ran his fingers through his hair in frustration.

"No, where is she?" The concern was heavy in Ridge's voice. "I'll call the boys to help look for her. We'll stay here and wait on them."

Within ten minutes Oakley and Chase were pulling up, jumping out of the truck. "We brought a search light to scan the sides of the road." Chase said as he climbed into the back of Ridge's truck. Oakley got in the back of Dalton's truck. They went in opposite directions, scanning the sides of the country road.

It took them about twenty minutes to locate where she went off the road. Chase saw ruts in the side of the ditch. He hit the roof of the truck.

"Ridge, look at the deep scrapes in the edge of the road. Looks like someone ran off the road." He walked over to the edge of the road, shining the light into the trees, seeing her truck. "There she is, call an ambulance."

Chase ran to the truck, calling her name, but no response. "Maggie..." It was all he could get out as he tried to open her door, but it was jammed.

Ridge ran around the other side of the truck, opening the passenger door. "She's bleeding from a gash in her forehead." He unbuckled her seatbelt, gently laying her back against the seat. They heard Dalton's truck come to a halt.

"How is she?" Dalton was at the side of the truck in no time. Ridge moved out of the way so Oakley could check her.

"She's alive, but the we need to get a blanket. Her body temperature is low." He pulled his jacket off, placing it across her. "Did you call an ambulance?"

"Yes, they're on the way." Ridge said as he walked around to the driver's side, trying the door again. Dalton walked over, yanking on the door several times, finally getting it open.

He wrapped his arms around her, trying to warm her as best he could without moving her too much. Oakley was afraid she might have neck or spinal injuries.

"Baby, hold on. The ambulance is on the way." He kissed her cheek.

Ridge and Chase paced beside the road, waiting on the ambulance. They were worried about her body temperature being too low and the head injury. Oakley had her head wrapped in the scarf he found on her seat.

The sirens and lights filled the cab of the truck as the ambulance arrived. They had to convince Dalton to leave her side so the medics could work with her. A back board was brought over and they carefully pulled her from the truck. By the time they had her in the ambulance and shut the doors, Dalton was going crazy with worry.

Ridge drove him to the hospital with Chase and Oakley following. Oakley called their parents and Luke. They prayed on the way as they followed the ambulance.

Chapter 5

The wait was hard, not knowing how bad it was. Oakley kept reassuring them that it was possibly just a concussion and slight hypothermia. But they still paced as they waited. Dalton stood at the window, staring out with a blank look.

As soon as the doctor walked in, Dalton was beside him. "How is she?"

"Calm down Dalton." The doctor smiled, "Your bride will be able to walk down the aisle. She has a slight concussion, but you guys reached her in time. I want to keep her overnight, just for observation. Also, make sure she takes it easy for a couple days."

"Thanks. When can we see her?" Dalton said before anyone could response. It brought a snicker from everyone at his insistence.

"They're placing her in a room now, so the nurse will come get you once she's settled in." He shook the hands that were extended with a smile. Then he looked back at Dalton. "By the way, you're the first one she asked for."

Dalton grinned sheepishly as he put his hands in his pockets. His heart warmed at the thought of her asking for him before her family. It spoke volumes.

Chase put his arm across Dalton's shoulders. "Maggie is a strong willed woman. She wouldn't let a small thing like an accident keep her from the wedding. If I know my sister, she'll be begging to go home tonight." He winked at Mrs. Cauthen as he spoke.

"I'm just glad she's alright." Mr. Cauthen

said as he poured a cup of coffee.

A few minutes later the nurse told them to go back for a few minutes. Dalton was the first on at her side, leaning down to kiss her lips. She smiled, then frowned when it made her head hurt.

"Hey baby. How do you feel? What happened? Can I do anything for you?" His questions came in rapid fire succession as he grasped her hand tightly.

"Dalton, take a breath. I'll be alright. I love you so much." Maggie put her other hand on top of his. "Now, go tell the doctor I'm going home, today."

Oakley walked up to the other side of the bed. "Not a chance Mags. You'll do as the doctor said, that is if you want to be a hundred percent for the wedding day." His words made her lay back again.

"OK, OK. I'll stay." Maggie's frustration showed through as she rolled her eyes with a dramatic flair.

The family each kissed her before they headed home to get some sleep. Dalton sat down in the chair beside the bed. "I'm staying with you until time to go home."

"Dalton, you don't have to do that." She smiled as he pulled his chair close to the bedside, holding her hand to his lips.

"We're about to be husband and wife, so how would that look if I left you when you need me the most?"

"I'm glad you're staying." She snuggled down in the blanket, feeling the sedative starting to take effect.

"By the way, what happened tonight?" He watched her eyes growing heavy.

"A deer darted in front of me and when I swerved to miss her, I lost control. The next thing I knew; I woke up in an ambulance." Her eyes were closed now, but she mumbled. "I love you Dalton..."

"I love you too baby. I'm so glad you're

alright. Life wouldn't be worth living without you." He kissed her as she drifted into a deep sleep. As he sat and watched her sleep, his heart slowed down. When he'd seen her truck bent around that tree and then her unconscious, his heart went into overdrive.

It was around eight in the morning when she woke with a splitting headache. Groaning as she opened her eyes, the lights bothering her. Dalton was at her side within a second.

"Baby, what do you need?" He held her hand, rubbing the back with his thumb.

"My head is pounding." She reached up, touching her aching forehead. The bandage and stitches prevented her from rubbing it as she'd wanted to do. "I hope these stitches are out by the wedding."

Dalton stood up, then leaned over to look her in the eyes. "All I care about is that you'll be at the wedding. The bandage or the stitches, they don't matter, all that matters is you're alright." He sat on the edge of the bed, careful not to jostle her too much. "You gave me quite a scare. Every time I shut my eyes, all I see is your truck crumpled and you laying against the steering wheel."

Maggie's eyes filled with tears. "I wanted these last two weeks before the wedding to be so special." Her bottom lip trembled as she held in the emotions.

He couldn't help but laugh. "Baby, any day with you is special. I love you." Leaning forward, he kissed her with such tenderness that the tears she'd held, flowed down her cheeks.

The doctor walked in, clearing his throat. "Alright you two, wait for the wedding."

Dalton looked up, "Her head is pounding. Is that normal?" Concern creased his brow.

Flipping open the medical chart, "Yes, that's normal." His attention went to Maggie. "You took quite a bang on the head. It only took a couple of stitches, but they should be out before you walk down the aisle. As for the headache, you had a slight concussion. Usually the headache eases in a day or two."

"I have so much to do, can I go home now?" Maggie went to sit up, but slumped back against the pillow.

"I'm letting you go around lunch, but you're to rest for a couple of days." He wrote something in her chart, then closed it. "Don't make me call your brothers, so listen to my words, rest."

"She will rest, even if I have to tie her to the bed." Dalton said in a serious tone.

The doctor gave her a pat on the shoulder. "I think he's serious, so I would listen."

"But I have so much..." She didn't finish her sentence when Dalton's intense gaze. "Alright, alright! I'll rest, but only long enough to get over this headache." She sighed in frustration as the two men grinned at one another. They both knew she'd be running around in no time, doing the exact opposite of what she should be doing.

Dalton called her parents to let them know he'd be bringing her home a little after lunch. Then he sat back, propping his booted feet up to take a nap. Maggie watched him sleep. He lightly snored as sleep consumed him. She giggled as she thought of waking him during the night to quiet him. Soon they'd be husband and wife. He was already showing her how much he cared by staying with her. It touched something deep inside of her.

Chapter 6

Maggie spent the next two days resting as per the doctor's instructions. She tried to get out of it, but between Dalton and her watchful family, she had no choice. Laying around all that time made her antsy to get out. By the time her so called quarantine was over, she was almost crazy.

Mrs. Cauthen took the time to decorate for Christmas. She wanted to surprise her daughter with all the new decorations of white. The tree was almost ten-foot-tall in all its glory. It was adorned with all the treasured Cauthen ornaments that the children made over the years. The Christmas balls were all white and red, accented by white poinsettia blossoms dotting the tree. It was like something out of a dream.

The mantle was covered in snow, with red candles in silver candle holders. Above the mantle hung a large wreath that was made of greenery, red shiny ornaments and white ribbon. Everywhere you looked, there was a memory of Christmas past. Over the years, Bridget had collected many things to make the house glow with Christmas cheer.

Each piece of Christmas held a special memory. There was the Santa and his wooden sleigh that had been Grantland's parents. Then she placed the hand painted nativity that Maggie did when she was twelve.

She unwrapped the Christmas balls that Grantland helped the kids make when they were small. Each child's handprint was on one side and their name and date on the other. As she hung each one on the tree, the memories of her children came flooding in. When she got to Maggie's a tear slipped from her eye. The handprint was tiny. She was only two when they made them. Now she was getting married.

As soon as Maggie stepped out of her room, the smell of scented candles and simmering spices assailed her senses. She smiled as she made her way down the garland covered stairway. The den was beyond beautiful and she could imagine her wedding. It was like a dream.

Mr. Cauthen found her in front of the tree, gazing up at the white, flowing angel on top. Her smile was the sweetest he'd ever seen. His heart swelled with pride as he watched her face light up with happiness. He was proud of all of his children and knowing she was marrying a man of honor made him happy.

She looked just like her mother had at the same age. It was amazing how much alike they were.

"I'm glad to see you up and around munchkin." He said as he put his arms around her in a hug.

"Thanks dad. It's good to be up." Placing her hands on his arms as they stood looking at the tree. "Mom did a great job."

"She always does. Christmas is her favorite time of year."

"Has she always loved Christmas?" Maggie asked, looking up at him.

"As long as I've known her, which is most of her life. She's always filled this house with Christmas cheer. Even our bathroom has a tree." He shook his head in amazement. "But I wouldn't take that from her for nothing in the world. It's her way."

"I can't wait to walk down the stairs on your arm and marry Dalton."

"He's a good man. I couldn't have picked a better man for my baby girl." He hugged her tighter, then walked over to put another log on the fire.

"I've always loved him in one way or another. Even when I was little, I had a crush on him. Funny, now he'll be my husband." She reached out to touch an ornament that Ridge made when he was little. It held a picture of him. The smile that touched her lips was of love. Her family was her heart.

"The house will be empty soon. It will be strange having all of you married and out of the house." Grantland put his hands in his pockets as he looked down at the fire crackling back to life.

Maggie's expression changed to one of sadness. "It will be hard leaving this home. But Dalton and I will make a home together."

"You're always welcome here, but you know that." He said as he touched the tip of her nose. "I'm going down to the barn to help Chase."

"I'll go with you." She followed him out, grabbing her big coat.

Chase gave her a hug as she walked into

the barn. "Hey sis. How's the noggin?"

"Better, but the stitches itch." She reached up to pat the area on her forehead.

"I think Star misses you. She's a little off the food at the moment."

Maggie went over to stroke her horses nose. "I missed you too girl. As soon as I can, we'll go for a long ride, I promise."

"But not until the doctor releases you." Oakley said as he walked out of the next stall. "That's an order."

"Meanie." She said, sticking her tongue out at him, childishly.

"That was mature for someone getting married next week." Oakley touched her cheek, then looked at her stitches. "Looks like your forehead is healing nicely."

"The doctor said the stitches will be out in five days."

"At least they'll be out before the wedding. What did the insurance say about your truck?" He reached out to give Star a scratch behind the ear.

"It's totaled. I have to go shopping for a new truck, but Dalton wants me to wait until after the wedding." Shrugging, Maggie put her arms around Stars neck. "I need the truck to finish my errands."

"You can use mine if you need to go anywhere today. I'll be busy watching over the birth of the foal. Lady is already laying down, so it shouldn't be too long."

He walked down the corridor of stalls, turning into the tack room, leaving Maggie with Star. She stood for a long while, talking soothingly with her horse. By the time she walked back to the house, Star was eating again. Ridge just shook his head. That horse really loved Maggie.

The family got together for dinner that night. Maggie sat holding Dalton's hand as she watched everyone passing food around, laughing and talking. It was loud, but wonderful. Dalton squeezed her hand, pulling it to his lips, then leaning to whisper in her ear.

"What's going through that pretty head?" His breath making her giggle as it tickled her neck.

"Just enjoying this moment with family. It's hard to believe we'll be married by this time next week."

"I can't wait." He growled, drawing another giggle from her.

Ridge watched the couple with a smile. It had been hard to accept their relationship. Dalton was too old for his little sister, but once he saw the love between them, how could he not be happy. Then again...

"OK, there will be enough time for that after the wedding." Ridge said in a gruff voice.

Maggie gave him a sweet smile. "Does it bother you big brother?"

"I have to say in all honesty, yes it does. It's hard to watch your baby sister necking right in front of you."

"They weren't necking, Ridge." Mallory said with a laugh. "We were worse than them, so get a grip on the big brother gene."

Dalton grasped Maggie's chin, bringing her face around to face him. He gave her a kiss that sent her mind reeling. This brought a moment of silence around the table. When he released her, his gaze met Ridge's.

"Now that was proper necking buddy. Try it sometime." His wink at Mallory brought laughter to everyone.

Ridge smiled, knowing he'd been bested. "Alright, that's enough."

That night as Maggie walked Dalton to his truck, the stars twinkled overhead. The night air was frosty with the threat of snow. She looked up, smiling.

"It's such a beautiful night." Maggie said.

"I only have eyes for you." He said, pulling her into his arms. "Get a good night's rest. Love you."

"Love you too."

        She watched him leave, sadly.

Chapter 7

The night before the wedding, the men took Dalton out for dinner and to celebrate his last night of being a single man. All of the Cauthen women stayed in, watching sappy Christmas romances and sipping hot cider. Maggie's nerves were taking over as she climbed into her bed for the last time. She looked around the room, feeling nostalgic.

Above the bed was a tiny hole where she'd thrown a marble up to see if it would stick. Looking over at the window, she smiled remembering Luke breaking out a pane with a baseball. This room held so many memories. Snuggling down in the covers, she remembered Ridge sitting by her bed when she had the flu.

She'd had an amazing childhood. Even with four over protective brothers, she'd managed to have a good time. Most of the time she kept them in the dark about what she did, but they loved her anyway. Rolling to her side she giggled. Tomorrow she was marrying the man of her dreams. It was like a fairy tale. Reaching down, she pinched her side to see if she was dreaming, but it hurt, so this was really happening.

Sleep finally claimed her around two. Her dreams were filled with love and smiles. As the sun crept across her bed, waking her gently from sleep, she opened her eyes. The smile that spread across her lips was beautiful. Sitting up, she giggled again, remembering this was her wedding day.

A knock at the door had her head turning. The door swung open with Mallory, Cara, Ellen and Rachel bursting in. "Wake up young lady! You have a big day and we're here to get it started." Ellen said as she flopped down on the side of the bed.

"I'm in charge of your hair, Cara will do your nails, Mallory and Ellen will help with your wardrobe." Rachel sat down, hugging Maggie.

"Thank you so much. I can't believe I'm actually marrying Dalton today." She lay back with a sigh.

Ellen winked at her, "He is a hunk. You're a lucky lady."

Maggie looked over at her sister in law. "I am a lucky lady." A giggle burst from her again making the others laugh out loud.

"You need some breakfast." Mallory walked out the door, bent down and picked up a tray laden with croissants and coffee. "A breakfast fit for a queen."

They sat down and everyone ate a croissant as they talked about the day to come.

Mrs. Cauthen stood in the doorway watching her girls. She was honored to have all of them in her life. Her sons had picked their wives well. Then her gaze went to her daughter as she laughed with her friends. Today her baby girl would leave the nest, it was a great day, but a sad one.

Maggie looked up in time to see her mom wipe a tear. "Oh, mom, come join the fun."

Bridget Cauthen was a beautiful woman. She didn't look her age, not even a little. As she sat down on the bed with the others, she smiled, raising her coffee cup.

"This is to all the weddings before and the one today. May it bring you much joy and happiness." She almost choked on the sob that escaped her lips.

After their breakfast, the ladies rushed Maggie into the bathroom for a shower. Then the festivities began. Everyone worked together to push the furniture in the den to the walls. The guys brought in white chairs and the women put white satin slip covers over each one. Rachel tied decorative red bows on each chair, Letting the ribbon flow into the floor.

The wedding was planned for three and as the time drew near, Maggie began to shake with nerves. With all the flurry of activity all morning, her nerves had stayed hidden, but now as Rachel curled her hair, she was a mess.

Dalton dressed at Oakley's house with the other men. He couldn't make a correct sentence as his nerves took his words away. Ridge put his hand on Dalton's shoulder with a laugh.

"It's like this for every man as they take the plunge, but believe me, once she starts toward you, all of that will fade away. The only thing you'll think about is her." Ridge said with a smile.

"She's all I think about anyway. I guess I'm afraid that I'll mess things up. Maggie is so special and I'm one lucky man that she said yes. I'm not worthy by a long shot."

Mr. Cauthen walked over with

encouraging words. "If you weren't worthy, Maggie wouldn't have given you a second look. That daughter of mine has loved you for as long as I can remember. She's also the most driven person I know, so believe me when I say this, she knew exactly what she was doing when she said yes."

Dalton pulled at his tie, feeling like it was choking him. "Is it hot in here?"

Chase snorted with laughter. "It will get hotter as the day goes on. Just wait until you see her for the first time, you'll think your body will explode."

Ridge swung around at his brother's words, "Chase! He's marrying our sister, so don't remind us about his feelings about her." He ran his hands over his face.

"We all knew that one day she'd get married, but it's hard to think of our little sister..." Luke's words dropped off as all heads swung in his direction. "You know what I mean. It's hard to think of her leaving Five Oaks, out of our careful watch."

All of them sighed, realizing for the first time that she was all grown up. It had been their job, or so they thought, to keep her safe all her life.

"From the moment she was born, it was like she was your angel. All of you have been great brothers, a little over protective at times, but the love all of you share is something special. I still can't believe how easily you all accepted this marriage." Mr. Cauthen said, giving each of them a look of respect.

"I'm still in shock that I haven't been shot or kidnapped and taken to a remote island somewhere." Dalton said as he leaned on the wall watching his new family just being themselves. He's always loved this family and envied what they had.

"It's still an option. We have about thirty minutes to figure out which island. What do you think guys?" Chase looked over at his brothers with a smirk.

"I think somewhere warm, maybe the Caribbean." Oakley said as he put his arm around Dalton's shoulders. "Lucky for you, we like you. But now it's time for the brotherly advice." He looked at Dalton in seriousness. "Be good to her or you'll deal with all of us. I think you get the idea."

"She'll never shed a tear by my hand. I'll move heaven and earth to make her the happiest woman in the world." Dalton straightened his shoulders. "Now, let's go get this done. I have a bride waiting for me."

Chapter 8

Maggie walked down the stairway, a vision in white. Her dad waited at the bottom, reaching out his hand to grasp hers warmly.

"My beautiful daughter, you look like an angel." He leaned forward and kissed her cheek, then pulled the veil over her face. "I love you sweetheart. Remember Five Oaks will always be your home."

The sweet smile that she turned up to him was returned with the same eyes. Out of all the Cauthen children, she looked the most like Grantland.

"Thank you for the greatest childhood. Five Oaks will always be in my heart." She kissed his cheek in return. Then as the door to the den opened she smiled as her four brothers walked out to meet them.

Ridge extended his hand to her, "We each want to be a part of giving you to Dalton." He lifted the veil, kissing her cheek. Then he walked her to the doorway. "Be happy Maggie. He's a good man and I know he'll protect you as we would want, but if you ever..." His words drifted away as Oakley stepped up.

"I'll walk you over the thresh hold sweet girl." Oakley used the old nick name he'd called her as a child. Tears formed in her eyes as she gazed up at him.

Oakley handed her hand to Chase just inside the doorway, "And I'll walk you another foot, but know that I love you and will always be here for you." He squeezed her hand and lifted it to his lips. A single tear escaped her lashes. Chase wiped it away. "No tears today."

Then Luke took her other hand, leading her to where she could see Dalton. A light gasp escaped her lips as he came into view. "I love you, sis." He handed her to their father again.

It was the most precious gift her brothers could give her. She stood still for a moment watching them take their place beside Dalton. They smiled at her, giving her their blessings in that one gesture. The tears stopped as she looked back at Dalton, he was rakishly handsome standing there in front of the tree.

Her dad walked her to where her mom stood, tears streaming down her face. Maggie handed her a single long stemmed red rose and gave her a hug.

"You look beautiful." Mrs. Cauthen said through her tears.

Maggie couldn't manage any words as the emotions of the day were taking over. When she turned, Dalton was smiling his dazzling way, his eyes dancing with love. She was drawn to his side as her father relinquished her to her soon to be husband.

They turned, facing one another as he grasped her bouquet, handing it to Rachel. Then he grabbed her hands, pulling them to his lips as he kissed the back of both. He leaned in toward her to whisper, "I'm one lucky man and I can't wait for this to be over with so I can have you all to myself."

She giggled in response to his words. Then she looked up into his eyes, the love that she saw there was beyond anything she'd ever seen. Why had she been concerned about leaving Five Oaks? Here was her future, not Five Oaks as she'd always thought. Today she was marrying her best friend, the man that filled her every thought.

The minister started the ceremony as the couple turned to face him, still holding hands. Dalton squeezed hers gently as she began to shake.

Christmas ornaments were passed out to everyone before the ceremony. Each one came up to put them on the wedding tree. They were memories that the attendee had of the couple. It was such a sweet part of the ceremony. The last two ornaments would be put on after the ceremony.

A snicker erupted from one of her brothers as she made a mess of repeating her vows, bringing a stern look from their mother, but a grin from Maggie. Rachel handed her Dalton's wedding band and she slipped it over his tanned finger as she repeated the words of the minister. Then Ridge handed Maggie's to Dalton. He put the ring on her finger, then kissed it with a devilish grin.

The ceremony was traditional, but Maggie and Dalton added some of their own vows. As they held hands, each said the words they'd written. By the time they were done, both of them had tears in their eyes.

"The couple will now put their ornaments on the tree as a symbol of their love." The minister said as he handed the two hearts to Dalton. Maggie grabbed hers and together they joined them into one ornament. Each held a side of the ornament, placing it in the front of the tree among the others. Then they moved back to where they'd stood.

As the minister said for Dalton to kiss his bride, all he could think about was the honeymoon. "It's about time." Turning to her four brothers, he grinned. "Cover your eyes."

The room erupted in laughter as Dalton pulled Maggie's veil back, kissing her with a promised passion that made her toes curl up. When he released her, but only slightly, she was breathless.

They were announced as husband and wife. Dalton led his new bride down the makeshift aisle toward the reception. Maggie was glad they'd decided on a very small, intimate wedding.

Everyone was able to stand in the large formal dining room as the couple made a toast, then cut the three tiered cake. It was white with red poinsettias made out of fondant.

The Cauthen ladies made all of the refreshments. Most from the Cauthen family cookbook. Mrs. Cauthen's famous lemon pies, creamy pumpkin pies and light as a whisper tea cakes graced the table. Mallory toasted sugar and cinnamon pecans. Ellen baked cheese straws and sugar cookies in the shapes of Christmas trees. Cara made haystacks, and Rachel made mini pecan pies and wedding cookies. It was quite a spread.

Maggie stood beside Dalton, watching the family enjoy the celebration. Dalton pulled her close. "I love you Mrs. Sanders."

She smiled, enjoying the sound of her new last name. Reaching up, she pulled his face to hers. "And I love you Mr. Sanders." The kiss she gave him was long and had someone clearing their throat behind them.

Dalton looked around to see Ridge standing beside them. "Can't you two wait until the honeymoon?" He groaned and walked past them to get some punch.

"Nope, I can't." Dalton said making Maggie giggle.

For the next thirty minutes they posed for what seemed like thousands of pictures. By the time the photographer said she was done, Dalton and Maggie were sagging. Rachel went upstairs with Maggie to help her change, while Dalton went to the guest room to change into jeans. They met at the bottom of the stairs. He was in jeans and a button down, she was in her jeans and a sweater.

Maggie hugged her family as they prepared to go to the bed and breakfast in town for the first night, then they'd catch a flight in the morning to the Montana. Dalton helped Maggie put her jacket on, then after he had his on, they walked out the front door to the cheers of their family and friends. As they ran to the waiting truck, everyone threw bird seed.

Once they were inside the truck, Dalton kissed her, then put the truck in drive. "Well, we're on our way. Are you ready for your new life?"

Maggie grabbed his hand, "I've been ready since we were kids."

That night as they held one another in the antique canopied bed, life began for them. Maggie was happy beyond words, and Dalton felt as though he'd burst from contentment. He reached over to the bedside table and handed her a small wrapped gift.

She grinned, "What's this?" Sitting up to unwrap the gift.

"It's your Christmas gift." He watched her eyes light up when she pulled a key chain out that held two keys.

"One is for our house and the other is for

your new truck." He waited for it to sink in.

Turning to look at him, then down at the keys and back at him. "What truck? I have a new truck?"

"Yes, baby, you have a new truck waiting for you at our house. I got with the insurance company and everything is taken care of."

She squealed and landed on him, kissing him with glee. He laughed between kisses. His new wife was exuberant and exciting. It was one of the things he loved about her.

Their life was starting out with happiness and love. As the moon rose over the world, they shared their love. It was a magical night...

Epilogue

Three Years Later

Mr. And Mrs. Cauthen sat on the hearth, holding their new grand babies. Maggie and Dalton's twins were born on Thanksgiving day. Ridge and Mallory had a two-month old daughter, Eve. She was sleeping in her father's arms as Beau ran around playing in with his new truck.

As they sat there, looking at their children and grandchildren, it warmed their hearts. The love they'd shared had multiplied into a family bursting with love and happiness. Each of their children were in love and happy. They'd chosen the right person to share their lives with and it made them feel like they'd raised them right.

Oakley and Ellen's oldest, Emma was sitting beside her mother, watching her two-month old sister taking her bottle. Oakley held their one-year-old son as he slept soundly. Ridge and Oakley had made a bet on whose daughter would be born first, since they announced their pregnancies at the same time. Of course Ridge's daughter was born ten hours before Oakley's.

Chase and Cara had a ten-month old son. He was sitting at his grandfather's feet, playing with some blocks. Mr. Cauthen reached down to ruffle his dark hair. It was evident he would be a true Cauthen.

Luke and Rachel had two-year-old triplets, three boys. They also had a one-year-old daughter and Rachel was pregnant with another girl.

The Cauthen family had grown with love and numbers. As they sat talking, laughing and enjoying the company, a new generation was growing up to be a close family. Five Oaks Ranch would thrive for generations to come because of the love that started with Grantland and Bridget Cauthen.

Cauthen Family Recipes

Icebox Lemon Pie

1 can of Eagle brand milk
2 lemons
2 eggs
1 teaspoon of salt
1 teaspoon of sugar
Vanilla Wafers

Grate lemons, add egg yolks beaten, salt, sugar, milk put over crumbled crackers with whole ones on the edge of pan for crust. Add beaten whites put in stove and brown

Pecan Pie

1 cup of syrup

1/2 cup of sugar

4 tablespoons of butter

3 eggs

1 teaspoon of vanilla

1 cup of pecans

Cook syrup and sugar together until thick. Beat eggs until light without separating pour over then hot syrup add butter and flavoring-pour into uncooked pastry. Drop nuts over top, put in hot oven for few minutes then reduce heat to medium and cook until pastry is done and pastry firm.

Tea Cakes

3 eggs

1 teaspoon vanilla

1 1/2 cups sugar

1 stick margarine and a small lump of Crisco

Mix the above and work in enough flour until you are able to roll it out, cut and bake at 325 degrees F or 350 degrees F till they are lightly brown.

Sugar and Cinnamon Pecans

Preheat to 275 degrees F. Pour butter into medium bowl and mix and pecans. Stir until the pecans are well coated. Arrange coated pecans in a single layer on one or two medium baking sheets. Bake in preheated oven for 1 hour stirring occasionally. Coat in cinnamon-sugar to taste.

Cheese Straws

Makes about 5 dozen

1/2 cup (1 stick) of room temperature butter

2 cups of room temperature sharp cheddar cheese

1 1/2 cups of all-purpose flour

1 teaspoon of salt

1/4 teaspoon cayenne pepper

Preheat the oven to 300 degrees F. In the food processor, add the butter, cheese, flour, salt, and cayenne and process until a smooth dough is formed. Scoop it into a cookie press Whit a flat ridged tip. Pipe the dough in 2-inch strips onto a lightly greased cookie sheet. Bake for 10 to 15 minutes or until lightly browned. Remove to racks to cool.

Sugar Cookies

Makes about 12 cookies

1/2 cup granulated sugar, plus 2 tablespoons

3/4 cup unsalted butter, (1 1/2 sticks)

1 teaspoon baking powder

1 teaspoon salt

2 1/3 cups all-purpose flour, plus 2 tablespoons

1 large egg

1 teaspoon vanilla extract

Sift together flour, salt, and baking soda in a medium bowl. In the bowl of a standing mixer with a paddle attachment, combine butter and sugar, beat on medium speed until light and fluffy. Add egg and vanilla and beat until combined. Add flour in 2 batches, scraping the bowl after each addition. Beat until dough comes together. Be careful not to over mix. Turn out the dough onto a lightly floured surface. Form the dough into a ball, wrap it in plastic, and refrigerate for 30 minutes. Place the dough in between 2 pieces of parchment paper and roll into 1/4 inch thick. Keep the dough in the parchment, transfer to cookie sheet and place in the refrigerate for at least one hour. Preheat oven to 350 degrees F. Cut cookies into desired shapes and place onto half sheet pan lined with parchment paper or an ungreased non-stick cookie sheet at least an inch apart. Transfer to freezer and let chill for at least 15 minutes or until they are stiff. Bake until cookies are light golden brown, about 10 minutes. Let cookies cool before decorating.

Haystacks

3 tablespoons of butter
40 large marshmallows
1/2 bag of chocolate morsels
6 cups of Golden Grahams cereal

Melt butter in a large pot. Add marshmallows stir constantly until melted. Add chocolate chips stir until melted. Add cereal stir until well coated. Pour into 13x9 baking dish or pour onto parchment paper and roll until 1/2 inch thick. Let cool and cut to size.

Creamy Pumpkin Pie

About 8 servings

3 ounces of softened cream cheese

1 tablespoon of cold milk

1 tablespoon of sugar

1 1/2 cups whipped topping

1 baked (9-inch) pie shell

1 cup milk

2 (4-ounce) can pumpkin

Whipped topping garnish

Pumpkin pie spice to taste

Combine cream cheese, 1 tablespoon of milk, and sugar in a bowl, whisk until smooth. Fold in 1 1/2 cups of whipped topping. In a separate bowl, combine 1 cup milk and pudding mix, whisk for 2 minutes or until well blended. Let stand for 3 minutes. Add pumpkin and pumpkin pie spice to taste. Combine all ingredients and mix until creamy. Pour into baked pie shell. Chill for 2 hours or longer. Pipe additional whipped topping around the edge of the pie.

Wedding Cookies

2 cups butter and margarine (2 sticks butter, 1 cup margarine)

1 cup sugar

5 cups flour

1 cup chopped nuts

1 tablespoon vanilla (if desired)

Mix butter and sugar until creamy, add flour and nuts and work well, pinch off walnut size pieces, roll into a ball. Bake at 350 degrees till lightly brown, then roll in powdered sugar.

Cauthen Family Tree

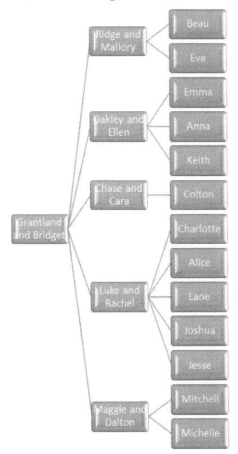

ABOUT THE AUTHOR

Stephanie Payne Hurt has been writing stories since she was a teenager, but only started publishing her work in 2012, 30 years later. The romance genre drew her in at an early age. Since 2012 she's published over 15 Romance novels/novellas. Stephanie is a busy lady. She's a Children's Minister, Accountant, wife and mother along with a blogger and writer. Also she started a publishing service called Horseshoe Publishing alongside her editor and assistant. It's been an exciting ride and she looks forward to what the future holds for her writing. Currently she writes romance ranging from Christian, Contemporary, Suspense and Cowboy. Her work is available at many online retailers, on her website and in a bookstore in Zebulon, Georgia near her home.

Come by and visit her at http://www.stephaniehurtauthor.com/ subscribe to get updates and release dates, also her monthly newsletter! Also join her Street Team!

Connect with Author:

Twitter: @StephanieHurt4
Email: stephaniehurt4@gmail.com
Facebook: https://www.facebook.com/StephaniePayneHurt
Please give a review and let her know what you thought!

By Stephanie Payne Hurt

Ghost Lover

Moonbeam and Roses

A Love Never Lost

Finding the Right Time

Open the Heart

Safe in the Pirate's Arms

Finding Love, Later (Coming in 2016, New Series)

Series

Flames of Love

Tender Flames

Rekindled Flame

The Winner

The Winner is Love

The Winner Takes All

Women of Magnolia Hill

Victoria

Emma Rose

Lean on Him

With All My Heart

Faith through the Tears

Her Wish for Christmas

Five Oaks Ranch

Ridge

Oakley

Chase

Luke

Maggie

A Christmas to Remember

Made in the USA
Columbia, SC
26 September 2022